AF479833

This book belongs to:

Smile!

A Children's Book

BY DUC CHUNG & JAMES SIMMONS

Illustrated by Blueberry Illustrations

Dedication

This book is dedicated to all children
learning to read for the first time.

There are many reasons to smile.

You smile when you are happy.

You smile when you are nervous

...and when you are shy.

You smile when you wake up to a bright sunny day

...and excited for your first day of school!

You smile when you make new friends
Come, come, Jimmy...Welcome to the First Grade!
Ms.Smo
Jone

...and learn new lessons from your teacher.

Now class, let's learn our ABCs!

Ms. Smock's First Grade Class

A B C

You smile when you are at recess

...and get to slide down the tallest slide!

You smile when you get on the school bus to go home

...and your dog licks your face when you come home.
How was your first day, Jimbo?
I had an awesome day, Daddy!

You smile when you finish all of your homework

...and all of your chores.

You smile when your friends come over to play

...and eat a hearty dinner with your family.

You smile when your mom and dad tuck you in for the night

...and read you a funny bedtime story.

You smile when you fall asleep under your favorite blanket

...and dream a sweet dream full of smiles.

Dr. Duc Chung is a hospice and palliative physician from Fresno, CA. He enjoys writing music and children's books to uplift the human mind and spirit. Outside of work, he also enjoys spending time with his two dogs, Boba and Waffles.

Dr. James Simmons is an internist and hospice physician from Fresno, CA. Outside of work, he enjoys playing tennis and spending time with his dogs.